Cob and the Kingdom

Written by: Leigh Ann Hughes

Illustrated by: Stephanie Weinger

Library of Congress Control Number 2022915347

Paperback ISBN 978-1-954175-58-7

Hardback ISBN 978-1-954175-59-4

Distributed by Tivshe Publishing

Printed in the United States of America

Visit www.tivshepublishing.com

This book is dedicated to my daughters, E, J, and C. You are my heart, my soul, my motivation, my world.

Credit also to my dear husband, who helped me come up with some corny names!

Once upon a time, in a land far, far away, there lay a small kingdom, tucked at the bottom of a mountain range, surrounded by corn fields. The villagers loved their home, but they were lonely. Blocked by mountains and cornfields all around, it was hard for anyone to come or go.

It was more than the mountains and cornfields blocking the villagers. At the bottom of one of the mountains, tucked away in a cave, lived a dragon. Although he never approached or attacked the kingdom, the people still feared him.

Too many knights sent by the king to deal with the dragon had returned, shaking with fear and having lost their battle gear.

Eager to keep their people happy, King Kernel and Queen Millie held huge festivals. The parties were enough to keep the villagers happy for a time, but once they ended, their loneliness returned. The king and queen saw the gloomy looks throughout the village and felt at a loss. They despaired for what to do.

King Kernel decided to try one last mission. A call went out for anyone willing to slay the dragon. In return, the king promised to give this person anything they desired. And of course, he promised to host the biggest party of all to celebrate the brave soldier's return.

But no one stepped forward. The people were too scared.

Finally, one brave man volunteered.

King Kernel and Queen Millie knew the man. He had come from a good home, though his parents had died young, leaving him alone. Forced to be on his own, he kept to his studies, and grew to be a strong and resourceful man. The king and queen were honored to have him represent the kingdom.

The man was knighted and given the name Sir Pop.

Another festival was held in honor of Sir Pop. Cheers were sent up for his successful trip and safe return. But to themselves, the people wondered if he would succeed.

The following morning, the villagers gathered to see Sir Pop off. The blacksmith presented Sir Pop with his best sword - to better slay the dragon - while children ran around, waving toy swords pretending to be Sir Pop.

Taking a deep breath, the knight waved to the crowd, his hand shaky with nerves. Then at last, he started on his journey.

For two days, Sir Pop trekked toward the base of the mountain. His hands shook as he thought of the brave knights who made this same trek before him and what scared them so. He knew, as afraid as he was, he needed to be brave and smart when he faced the dragon.

Eventually, the mountains were closer, and Sir Pop realized he was almost at the end of his path.

The cornfields thinned, and Sir Pop's fear took hold again. His eyes slowly scanned the area. Swords, shields, and other weapons lay spread out in front of him on the ground. Sir Pop wondered why the other knights had drawn their swords so far from the dragon's cave.

Sir Pop's hand moved to his own sword, but with great effort, he pulled it back. He would keep it in its scabbard until absolutely necessary. Maybe, just maybe, he thought, he might not need to use it.

Sir Pop continued on his way, this time at a slower pace. He knew the dragon would hear his approach, but hoped to delay as long as possible. If he was lucky, he would see the dragon before the dragon saw him.

The sounds of footsteps and rustling reached the dragon's ears as the knight moved through the cornfields. The dragon laid still, wondering if he should even go outside this time. But he knew he must. His claws curled into the dirt as he slowly stood up. Then, head ducked low, he slowly moved out of his cave.

Sir Pop stood still as the dragon appeared. The two eyed each other, both waiting for the other to make a move.

Seeing the dragon's head hang low, Sir Pop realized the truth.

The other knights had approached the dragon in fear, and so they had attacked first. The dragon had only been protecting himself and his home.

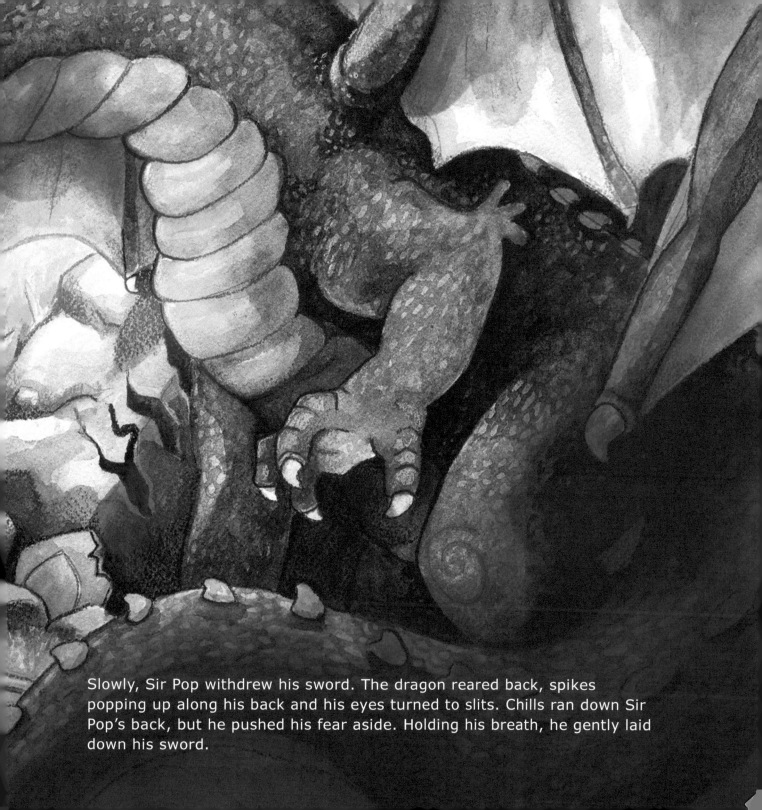

Slowly, Sir Pop withdrew his sword. The dragon reared back, spikes popping up along his back and his eyes turned to slits. Chills ran down Sir Pop's back, but he pushed his fear aside. Holding his breath, he gently laid down his sword.

Confused, the dragon set his feet back on the ground.

"Dear Dragon," the knight said, raising his arms in the air as he approached,

"I wish you no harm. My name is Sir Pop, and I have come to make a deal. If the people of my kingdom may pass with no harm from you, we will deliver no harm to you."

The dragon was astonished. He had only been approached with hatred before.

Pulling his spikes back in, the dragon cautiously replied, "Brave Knight, I wish you no harm either. All I wish is for some friends of my own. It is very lonely here."

Sir Pop's head dropped in relief. He could relate to the dragon's loneliness.

"The people of my kingdom are quite kind," he said. "Come back with me, and you will be met with the biggest and best party of all."

The dragon took a small step back, his claws curling into the ground again.

Finally, he said, "Sir Pop, I graciously accept your invitation. Thank you for your kindness. You may call me Cob."

The two set off for the kingdom at once. On the return trip, Sir Pop and Cob became fast friends, but as they neared the village, Sir Pop heard gasps and screams.

"All is well!" he shouted, waving his arms for attention. "He is a friend!"

Slowly, the villagers heard Sir Pop's calls and quieted, growing from a small frightened crowd to a larger confused but mesmerized one.

The next day, the kingdom held a party for Sir Pop, and now also for Cob. Sir Pop watched as the villagers hesitated to approach Cob. Though they were nervous, their fear disappeared when they saw how friendly he was. The children even climbed onto Cob's back and slid down his tail, begging for rides.

Cob was so happy to finally make friends that he sucked in a huge breath, and breathed fire…

...all over a corn field, making popcorn for the party!

Queen Millie gathered some women and children to collect the popcorn in bowls. King Kernel and Sir Pop gave big smiles to Cob, as he ducked his head and his cheeks turned red.

"Thanks Cob! That's a lot easier than us trying to build our own fires to pop it!" Sir Pop said. The two new friends shared a look knowing they wouldn't be alone anymore.

From then on, Cob was invited to the kingdom often. He spent a lot of time with Sir Pop, but he also helped King Kernel and Queen Millie plan the kingdom's travels. And the villagers were happy even when the king and queen weren't throwing festivals. Life was good for the small kingdom and the dragon. Even better, Cob always made popcorn for the festivals and balls.

Meet the Author

Leigh Ann Hughes

Leigh Ann Hughes is a happily married mother of three daughters and a rambunctious dog. Born and raised in the wonderfully small state of Delaware, she never imagined her life to grow any bigger than that. Being an avid reader all of her life, and even writing some as a young girl, she found that creativity again after the birth of her children. "Cob & the Kingdom" is just the start of her author journey. More books to come, ranging from picture to Elementary chapter to Middle School chapter books.

To learn more, visit her website at:

www.LA.writes4kids.com

Meet the Illustrator

Stephanie Weinger

Stephanie Weinger is a Children's Natural Sceince Illustrator whose lifelong passion for wildlife mixed with her desire to learn and to draw. She hopes to inspire children to learn about the world around them, while being kind, compassionate and curious about all creatures. "Cob & the Kingdom" is Stephanie's second published Children's Book. She is always looking for new books to illustrate and is even writing a few of her own!

To see more of her work, visit her website at:

www.stephweinger.com

CPSIA information can be obtained
at www.ICGtesting.com
Printed in the USA
BVHW022026101122
651686BV00002B/6